THE WITCHING TRAIL

THE OKRITH NOVELLAS
BOOK FOUR

A.K. MULFORD

NORTHERN COURT
Murreneir
Brufdoran
DRUNEHAN
Vurstyn
HIGH MOUNTAIN COURT
Valtere
YEXSHIRE
SWIFTHILL
SEA OF CALLIPHO
WESTERN COURT
Silver Sands Harbor
OKRITH

N
SEA OF WETAMUIR
...port
Falhampton
ROTTED PEAK
EASTERN COURT
WYNREACH
Haastmouth
SOUTHERN COURT
Crushwold
SAXBRIDGE

The red ribbon waved like a crimson sentinel amongst the verdant green. So high they had to crane their necks to see, that lone ribbon meant safety to any witch who spotted it.

Lysi scrambled down the trunk, dusting the bark off her tunic and giving Raffiel a nod. She stooped, lifting her weapons belt from the dirt and buckling it back onto her waist. One more ribbon waved in the breeze high above—one more beacon of hope.

Prasus pushed off the trunk where he waited for his daughter to descend the tree. "We shouldn't hang them any closer to Yexshire," he said. "The Northern soldiers will catch on to what we're doing."

"How many years has it been?" Raffiel mused with a chuckle. "They still haven't bothered to learn the witches' lore."

Lysi pulled a knife from her belt and began carving the Mhenbic symbols into the tree. *The snake and the oasis,* it read— a common story amongst the red witches. It told the tale of the snake that led a lost red witch over Mount Seripedes to an oasis in the Southern Court. It was a lesser mountain between the High Mountains' tallest summits, one only the people of the High Mountain Court bothered to learn the name of. All the humans, fae, and witches of the High Mountains knew that story and would recognize those symbols.

"How many people have found us from the witching trail?" Prasus' voice was scratchy and deep. The short gray coils of his hair and silver stubble peppering his jawline were the only indicators that he was not still in his prime . . . that, and his fully grown daughter.

Raffiel cast a glance back at his two road-weary comrades. Prasus had been his mother's head guard, Lysi training to take her father's place one day. Now, they were the only trained fae warriors left from the High Mountain guard.

"Why are we out here?" Lysi rolled her eyes. "If any remaining survivors can find us by following the trail?"

She brushed one of her thick black braids over her shoulder and rubbed her hand across the back of her neck. She looked so much like her father—both having incredibly muscular, warrior's bodies built through a lifetime of training. Lysi's warm brown skin was a shade lighter than her father's, more like her mother's. . . the last reminder Lysi had of her.

"We haven't searched the eastern slopes yet," Raffiel said. "There could be encampments beyond Yexshire, or people fleeing from other courts back into the High Mountains."

"We need to get out of this forest," Prasus countered. "Every second in the High Mountains is a second closer to you being captured by the North. Besides, there may be no more witches left out here."

"It's been years, Raf," Lysi grumbled, blowing the wood dust off her knife and sheathing it. "I think it's time to focus on those we've already saved."

Raffiel's two-person army, Lysi and Prasus, trained the other camp residents to fight, but only his guards were welcome on missions into the High Mountains. Too many people would draw attention and they needed to be stealthy. He knew Lysi would follow him back up and over the mountains as many times as he asked, but he had a nagging feeling in his gut that she was right. He already knew from the look in

Prasus' eyes the elder fae wanted to give him a lecture—probably something about his duty and destiny.

This is a job for a soldier, not for a King, Prasus had told him time and time again. *It's time to crown you. It's time claim your title, Raffiel.*

He gave Prasus a knowing nod, and his guard held his tongue. He knew Raffiel heard his constant reminder even without speaking it. But Raffiel wasn't ready to be the High Mountain King, not when the Northern King, Hennen Vostemur, still controlled Yexshire and the Immortal Blade.

Their little campsite was all that remained of his court now. Raffiel was just a fae without his ancestor's throne or talismans, unworthy to lead them.

"Come on," Prasus said, pulling Raffiel from his storming thoughts. "Let's go check the next ribbon hasn't been stolen by some nesting bird."

They trudged through the springtime forest. Green shoots poked from the cold earth and flower buds clung to bare branches. Soon, the forest would be awash with brilliant pastels and vivid greens, the High Mountains returning to life after another long winter.

Lysi's fingers trailed across the bushes. "We're a month too early for the berries," she grumbled. "We'll have to come back."

Prasus huffed, glancing at his daughter. "There's plenty of fruit in the Southern Court."

"It's not the same," she groused.

It wasn't the same. The food in the South was delicious, bountiful on every tree branch an arm's reach of their campsite . . . but it didn't taste like home. Even with the biting winter snow, the thin dry air, and the short growing seasons, the High Mountain Court still held its grip on Raffiel's soul. There was a rightness to all those things—the smells, the tastes, even the hardships. It felt right to be in this Court, and one day, he'd move his people back—to the place where their souls felt complete.

The landscape was rough and rugged, suiting the constitution of the people who called it home. They didn't revel like the Southerners, drinking to excess and partying until dawn. They were more stoic and thoughtful, though equally welcoming to all. They valued hard work and perseverance—qualities which had stood the survivors well over the past many years. If anyone could survive the ruin of their kingdom, it would be the people of the High Mountain Court.

Raffiel's boots scuffed along the path, his mind wandering to what the capital might look like after a rebuild. There would be plenty of jobs for builders, craftsmen, farmers . . . He would see to it that the debts of the other crowns were called in and they all pitched into the relief efforts. He cleared his throat. It was a daydream and nothing more. There would be no going back.

Something from the corner of his eye made him pause, and his soldiers instantly halted with him. It was so subtle he almost missed it, but it was there—the slightest peek of a cinnamon-brown cloak hiding behind the tall shrubs.

He whistled low, pointing a finger to the dense bushes. Stepping lightly across the leaves, he unsheathed his rusting sword from its scabbard. He took another step and steadied himself, preparing to spill blood.

CHAPTER TWO

With his sword pointed at the spiky bush, Raffiel commanded, "Show yourself."

Two pale hands instantly popped up in surrender, a mop of straw-blond hair following.

"Please, don't hurt me," the man pleaded.

The trembling man stood from his crouch. Impressively tall, he had a lined, weathered face despite his otherwise youthful appearance, like someone who had gone days without any sleep. His sky-blue eyes flickered to a deep shade of brown, bronze flames circling his fingertips.

A brown witch.

The tightness in Raffiel's chest eased. "It's just a brown witch," he called and heard his comrades sigh. It wasn't the type of witch they'd been searching for, but at least it wasn't an enemy ambush as he'd feared. Raffiel turned his gaze back to the nervously shifting man. "What is your name?"

"Oliver Doledir," the man said tentatively, wringing his hands together.

"Oliver." Raffiel tipped his head in greeting.

"You're . . ." The brown witch's eyes widened as he took in Raffiel's shaved head, brown skin, and pointed fae ears. "You're the crown prince of the High Mountain Court, aren't you? I thought all of the Dammacus line was dead." Raffiel's eyes saddened at the surprise on the man's face. "It makes sense now why King Vostemur can't wield the Immortal Blade."

Raffiel clenched his jaw as he sheathed his rusting sword—an inefficient, dented relic. If only he had managed to grab the Immortal Blade . . . his family's fortunes would've been very different that night if it hadn't been resting upon the altar of the temple a floor above. Why hadn't his mother worn it like the weapon it was designed to be?

He knew the answer: because she didn't think anyone would ever dare to challenge the High Mountain fae, let alone their allies to the north. Now, he needed to stay alive so that the Northern King wouldn't be able to wield the Immortal Blade against the rest of Okrith. The blood in his veins bound that sword to the Dammacus line, and if he fell, it would be freed. He was the only one left standing between Hennen Vostemur and the rest of the realm. It was yet another reason why Prasus didn't want Raffiel gallivanting off into the mountains on rescue missions. His only purpose in life was to survive, a lone stone holding back an entire dam.

"How did you end up here, Oliver?" Raffiel asked, trying to soften his imposing posture. He reached back to Lysi for a water skin.

Oliver eagerly drank as if he'd been days without water. He had that hollowed-out look about him—like he'd been one step too close to death. His eyes had a vacant flicker of horror. Raffiel knew what it was like to put himself into another world in order to survive what he had seen. This brown witch wouldn't be the first who'd fled from his own mind.

Oliver wiped his knobby hand across the back of his mouth. "Witch hunters, Your Highness."

"Just Raffiel," he corrected gently. There was no throne for him anymore. There was no castle. This was how he could help his people—giving them water, guiding them to safety. Whether Prasus wanted him to be King or not, this was all Raffiel cared to be.

"Raffiel," Oliver said carefully. His hands shook as he

returned the water skin. "They chased us into the woods on the border. I cut down through Silver Sands, but there were more coming in through the South. I ran, not knowing which way I was headed. I spotted the ribbons in the trees, noticed they were making a trail, and thought I'd follow them."

"It was a good thought," Raffiel said with a smirk. "But you're heading the wrong way. In another week you'd be in the middle of Yexshire, and I'm guessing you wouldn't want that?"

Oliver's eyes widened as he shook his head. "Those Northern soldiers will grab anyone they think might be a witch, red or otherwise."

"Did you not read the words carved in the trees?" Raffiel asked.

Oliver nodded. "The serpent and the stream?"

"Oasis," Lysi said, pointedly wiping the opening of her water skin with her sleeve. Raffiel gave her a disapproving look and she stopped.

Prasus resumed his usual position, leaning against a tree trunk. "Do they not tell witchlings that story in the Western Court?"

"If they do, I don't remember it," Oliver said. "There were not a lot of stories in my house after my father died." His eyes were incredibly wide as he stared into the forest. Despite being a brown witch himself, Oliver looked like he needed a healer. "Are you heading back along the trail?"

"Might I have a private word, Your Highness?" Prasus asked, making Raffiel and Lysi roll their eyes. He beckoned with his weathered hand like a scolding father. "Come on."

Oliver bowed his head as if he wouldn't listen, but witch hearing was so poor compared to the fae that they wouldn't have to go far to speak out of earshot.

They huddled in a circle, and Lysi whispered, "We should just point him in the right direction and let him go. The others will find him and help him once he crosses the border."

"We should accompany him back to the camp," Prasus countered. "Look at him. He's clearly unwell."

Oliver's eyes were closed, his head tilted as if he was savoring the birdsong. Everything about him was slightly off, like he wasn't fully in his body anymore. He certainly needed someone's aid.

"We came to look for *our* people, for High Mountain people," Lysi hissed. "He's just a lost Westerner. Soldiers won't give him a hard time once he gets to the South."

"We just spotted witch hunters only a few miles northwest of here," Prasus chided. "They could easily be circling the foothills as we speak, and they won't care what type of witch he is if they can make a bit of gold from him."

"You would abandon our mission?" Lysi scowled at her father, her braids splaying out from the sudden twist of her head.

"We may not find anyone on this mission. Would it be worth it then if the brown witch dies?" Prasus narrowed a look at Raffiel. "It's your decision, Your Highness."

"You always say 'Your Highness' when you want him to agree with you," Lysi groused, but Prasus kept his eyes locked on Raffiel.

With a long, frustrated sigh, Raffiel said, "We go with him." Lysi opened her mouth to protest, but he carried on. "And then we turn around and finish what we started," he promised her, adding, "Maybe the berries will be ripe by then."

The muscle in her jaw popped out; she was clearly frustrated but gave a begrudging nod.

"Come on, Oliver," Raffiel called, turning toward the brown witch. "We'll get you to safety."

"Th-thank you." Oliver sighed, his shoulders drooping with such relief that Raffiel knew he made the right decision.

Prasus spoke true—there may be no more red witches in the High Mountains. He couldn't gamble away a real person's life for ones that might not even exist.

Craning his neck toward the canopy, Raffiel looked back at the ribbon behind them. They'd set this trail on their first escape to the Southern Court, but Raffiel suspected there were many more of his people still scattered across the High Mountains. And so he and his guards started their mission: to get as many to safety as possible. In all of his searches, he kept a weathered eye out for one person . . . but had never found him.

"Of all the people I thought might help me," Oliver murmured, lifting his splintering bow and quiver over his shoulder. He followed closely, one step behind Raffiel. "I would've never guessed a fae Prince."

Raffiel chuckled, though the truth of those words stung. "The world is a strange place nowadays."

"Too true," Prasus muttered.

Most of Raffiel's life had been ease and merriment—such an arrogant assurance that life would carry on uneventfully in privilege and comfort. His stomach growled as he trudged onward. Never did he think he'd live off foraged food and muddy river water. Never did he think that leading his people would mean trekking over the dangerous summits of the High Mountains and erecting campsites . . . But here he was, the last Dammacus alive, following a trail of blood-red ribbons to a foreign kingdom.

CHAPTER THREE

They walked until the blue sky faded to black, the thick layer of clouds receding with nightfall, revealing a brilliantly blue waxing moon. Raffiel decided they should risk a fire. At the high altitude of Mount Seripedes, the temperature plunged to near freezing, and though the snows had melted around the foothills, the ground still bit with frost and the grasses hardened to ice.

He sat wedged between Lysi and Prasus while Oliver huddled across the fire from them. Oliver wrapped the blanket they'd given him tighter around his shoulders as he stared into the flames. Their normally endless conversation had been stilted with the brown witch trailing behind them. They'd needed to slow to half their normal pace that day, forgetting their fae strength and speed several times along their trek.

"Do you have any family in the South?" Raffiel asked, breaking through the silence. "Someone you can reach out to when we arrive at the border?"

"My eldest sister lives somewhere in the South, I think," Oliver murmured. "If she's still alive . . . . But I don't know where. I haven't spoken to her in decades."

"It would be worth asking around," Prasus offered as he picked at the sinewy jerky stuck in his teeth. "Lots of families are still reuniting after the Siege of Yexshire . . . or you could stay at the camp with us."

"I don't want to be a burden to you if I can make my own way." Oliver shook his head. "I'm sure you have many mouths to feed."

"We do." Raffiel added another log onto the fire, grateful they'd found some dry kindling in the damp springtime weather. "But we wouldn't turn someone away if they needed our aid."

"I'll be all right." Oliver lifted his gaze through the thickening flames. "I might have a way to help you, though."

Raffiel quirked his brow. "How?"

"I've been hearing whisperings in the fires of late," he murmured. Lysi shot him a questioning glance. Oliver tilted his head to the side, looking skyward, and Raffiel wondered what the brown witch heard in his mind.

"Are you sure you didn't hit your head a little too hard there, friend?" Lysi gave a bemused laugh.

"My grandmother wishes to speak with you," Oliver said more firmly to Raffiel. "She wants to assist you in your cause. With her magic, you could join forces. She's a very powerful witch."

"I'm sure my people could always use the aid of more brown witches—"

"She's not a brown witch," Oliver countered. "She's a violet witch."

"Bullshit," Lysi said.

Prasus reached behind Raffiel and nudged her shoulder in a silent reprimand.

Oliver frowned, tossing a twig into the fire. "It's true. Look." He lifted his hand, magical flames twisting around his fingers.

"Looks pretty brown to me," Lysi snickered.

"It's purple too, though, from my grandmother's line," he insisted.

They all squinted closer at his flickering magic, but the

night was too dark and it looked a shade of bronze, nothing purple about it.

"Here." Raffiel passed Oliver a strip of salted jerky from his pack. "You should eat something."

"I haven't made this up!" Oliver pushed, leaning in toward the fire. "She's shown me. I've seen it!"

"Settle down," Prasus said in his deep, rasping tone, and Oliver leaned back against the trunk behind him again. "We're not saying we don't believe you—"

"We're sort of saying that," Lysi muttered and braced for another swift tap from her father.

"It's entirely possible some of the other covens have violet witch ancestors mixed into their bloodlines . . ." Prasus gave Lysi a look, warning her to behave. "The eldest of violet witches still existed when I was a boy. It was not that long ago they disappeared."

"The violet witches will rise again," Oliver said with a confident nod, his eyes seeming suddenly clearer. "My grandmother will make sure of it." He dug into the deep pockets of his cloak and pulled out a stubby, white candle flecked in shades of black and deepest lilac. "If you ever want to summon her, you can contact her through this."

"Keep your candle, witch," Lysi said. "We have fae fire."

"But this candle will reach her directly," Oliver replied. "It's spelled to reach a specific person."

Raffiel's eyes softened. Whatever this man had been through, it had clearly been harrowing. He wouldn't be the first brown witch to sample his own elixirs either. "You should hang onto it."

"No." He rose and put the candle into Raffiel's pack. "Keep it. Please. And consider calling upon her. She can help you take back Yexshire."

Raffiel was about to open his mouth to refuse when Prasus shot him a look.

"Thank you," he said instead. If it comforted this confused witch, it seemed worth it.

A witch wouldn't win back Yexshire, let alone a violet one.

The violet witches had scented magic—candles, perfumes, and incenses—nothing strong or aggressive like the other covens. They were known for wearing crowns of flowers and making love potions and calming vapors. What would a violet witch do to wage war on the North? Throw flower petals at them?

Raffiel's gaze drifted over the crackling embers to the brown witch. "Rest, Oliver. We have a long trek to the camp tomorrow."

Oliver tucked the blanket around himself tighter and closed his eyes, exhaustion seeming to pull him under with ease. Raffiel looked between his guards, and they shook their heads. They'd seen it all, found every sort of person in the woods of the High Mountains, but this one had him worried. Even with the magic of fae fire, news did not always travel. It was possible Oliver would never find his sister, or even know if she was still alive. Too many families were ripped apart, never to be reunited, but Okrith was a smaller continent than it seemed, and he prayed that Oliver would find his family. Raffiel prayed he'd find that silver-haired fae who haunted his dreams too.

"I'll keep first watch," Lysi said, stoking the fire with a stick. "You early birds can take the morning."

Prasus chuckled, leaning his head back against the fallen log behind him. "Enjoy the stargazing."

The stars were incredibly bright up on the mountainside. Raffiel couldn't remember them ever being so clear, as if the Gods had pulled them closer just for them to see. As the moon shone her silvery-blue light down upon them, Raffiel thought about the red witches and their full-moon prayers.

He lifted his fingers, staring in concentration, trying to summon that red magic the ancient red witches had blessed his ancestors with, but there wasn't a single spark. He'd seen his mother do it, seen the red flames circling her fingertips and her eyes glow with witch magic. It had been incredible—a fae Queen with red witch power. But whatever blessing Mother Moon bestowed his ancestors, it must've ended with her. He had no clue how to summon the red flames.

Riv probably would've learned. His heart ached thinking of

his little brother, always with a history book in his hand, his happiest moments pouring over scrolls with ancient scrawls. Rivitus would have conquered the witch magic, a power of the mind and not the body. Raffiel had the brawn and fighting prowess, but Riv had the sharp cunning and wisdom of a ruler even as a child. They would've made a great pairing with Riv as his head councilor. His throat bobbed, the pain washing through him as if it were only yesterday. He'd watched the life fade from his little brother's eyes before the flames consumed the grand hall, watched the chaos as what they thought at first was a fire turn into an attack.

Lysi placed a hand on his shoulder, and he looked at her with welling eyes. She seemed to know, seemed to feel the sorrow seeping into the air.

"The Goddess who spun starlight and wove it into the heavens . . ." she murmured, beginning the tale.

Raffiel closed his eyes, listening to her soft voice. It was how they got through the darkness and the quiet moments when the memories seemed too large to fight away. They told each other stories, stories that had nothing to do with them and everything all at once, and the stories would heal them. He let Lysi's soft words guide him to sleep.

CHAPTER FOUR

The entire morning was a downhill trudge, and Raffiel's yearning for new boots grew more with each step. His feet would be bloodied with new blisters by the time they reached the camp that evening. It always mesmerized him how quickly the downhill slopes of Mount Seripedes changed into the jungles of the South. From this vantage point, the delineation was clear: as the mountain sloped into a gorge, the evergreen forests changed to teeming jungle. One side of the dry riverbed was a forest of pine and deciduous trees covered in dead leaves and new spring buds, the other was thick vines and dense, bright-green underbrush. Colorful birds sat amongst the canopy, watching them as if welcoming them to the Southern Court. Raffiel could almost feel its heat. Soon, the thin, cool air would be thick and humid. Only a little further, and they'd be safe.

Oliver had dawdled at the back of the group all morning, and Raffiel had to remind Lysi for the hundredth time that witches could not walk as fast as fae. The closer they got to the border, the slower Oliver seemed to move. He was murmuring to himself in Mhenbic when Lysi leaned in to Raffiel and said, "What is he doing?"

"He's probably praying," Raffiel chided, giving her a look. "Who knows what horrors he's been through?"

"I don't think his mind is fully with us," Lysi said as she tried to peek back over her shoulder.

Raffiel looked to see Oliver taking a small parcel out of his cloak. "Are you okay, Oliver?" he asked, eyeing the curious sphere of fabric.

Oliver looked up at Raffiel with bloodshot eyes. "Light the candle, call for help," he whispered.

Raffiel furrowed his brow. "Help for what? Oliv—"

Oliver threw the bundle into the sky, drawing his bow and arrow with sudden speed. "Light the candle!" he shouted as he released his arrow.

The arrow struck the parcel in the sky, an incredible shot. An explosion of purple powder erupted from the bundle, smoky violet reigning down upon them. Shouts rang out from across the hillside and galloping horse hooves thundered underfoot.

Raffiel's eyes widened at Oliver as he nocked another arrow and pointed it straight at Raffiel's chest. "What have you done?"

"Light the candle, call for the violet witches!" Oliver's voice trembled as he pulled back the bowstring. "Pledge yourself to her, and she will save you."

Prasus stepped in front of Raffiel. "What in the Gods' names?"

Oliver released his arrow and Prasus barked out a cry of pain as it shot straight through the meaty part of his thigh and into the earth behind them. Oliver moved to nock another arrow but was silenced by two mounted Northern soldiers. Raffiel just caught the sight of the hissing serpents carved into their shining armor before Lysi tackled him to the ground. Another arrow flew over his head, grazing through his hair as it flew past.

The first knight unsheathed his sword, lifting it to swing at Oliver.

"Look out!" Raffiel bellowed, but Oliver didn't move.

"Light the—"

The sickening swing of the sword silenced Oliver's words.

His eyes bugged as blood trailed from his lips and he fell to his knees. Raffiel didn't have time to watch him die, not as those knights circled them. Lysi and Prasus pivoted, their backs coming together to protect each other from all sides.

Shit. One mounted soldier maybe they could take, but two?

Just as the first one neared, a third rider emerged from the forest.

The purple mist filtered down the forest, blanketing them in a sickly cloying fog. Horses whinnied and the soldiers shouted muted cries as they barreled through the haze. The floral smoke burnt Raffiel's lungs and he spluttered out a cough.

When he blinked again, the battle was warped, time seeming to slow, and he felt still in his body and not at the same time. He didn't feel the breeze or sting of cold, he couldn't smell or taste the freshness of the forest anymore. And while he watched his two comrades battle, frozen, he saw another world through his mind's eye.

"What is this?" he breathed, looking around a castle. He felt the warmth of the hearth, smelled the spiced meats and fresh baked bread. His eyes landed on a King upon his throne, a golden crown atop his head.

His eyes flared. It was him.

"This is the future I could give you," a warm scratchy voice echoed through his mind.

He spun, searching the palace, even as his physical body remained firmly planted in the battle.

"Who are you?" he shouted, though he didn't form the words with his mouth.

"I am your salvation," the voice spoke. "I will give you a crown, King Raffiel, and all it will cost is your fealty to my kind."

"What is your name?" He searched the shadows of his vision but couldn't find her. He swiped his hand through the haze. "What magic is this?"

"The most powerful magic in all the realm," the voice whispered. "And it can be yours. You can wield my coven at your command, for your own glory. All you need to do is swear a blood oath to me, and I will give you everything your heart desires."

Raffiel's throat dried to sand. "A blood oath," he snarled. "I am not swearing a blood oath to a faceless witch."

"That wouldn't be wise, Princeling." The witch's tone soured, revealing the true venom hiding underneath.

"You'd threaten me into a blood oath?" he growled. "You'd let your grandson die needlessly in order to deliver this hare-brained message?"

"I have more grandsons." Her voice was mirthless and cold.

His vision twisted, his consciousness tugging back into his body as Prasus grabbed him by one arm, trying to drag him away.

"This is your last chance to save the High Mountain Court," the voice hissed. "What do you say?"

"I say no," Raffiel shouted into his mind just as Prasus thrust out with his sword, impaling a downed soldier through the throat.

"I'll only let you live long enough to regret that choice," the voice snarled.

A hissing pop, like a log crackling on a fire, and the smoke vanished from Raffiel's eyes. He once again felt the cold and smelled the fresh mountain air . . . and the metallic tang of blood.

At the sight of his two fallen comrades, the last of the Northern soldiers turned his horse and vanished into the forest. Prasus fell to the ground, holding his injured leg. Lysi dropped beside him, inspecting the wound.

Oliver's lifeless eyes stared up into the pale spring sky, his mouth still forming words Raffiel couldn't hear as the color drained from his face. A pool of blood seeped into the earth, steaming against the frozen ground.

Raffiel shuddered as Oliver's lips stopped moving.

"What the fuck was that?" Lysi shouted, staring in the direction of the fleeing soldier. Birds flocked from the canopy in the distance, signaling his thundering flight. Lysi turned her dark eyes on Raffiel. "What happened to you? You looked like you were in a trance."

"That smoke," Raffiel said. "It warped my mind, I . . . Did it not affect you the same?"

"I was a bit distracted trying to fight off *three* mounted Northern soldiers!" Lysi waved toward the waving distant trees. "The smoke tasted flowery and gross, but it didn't affect me."

"What did you see?" Prasus panted, ripping his trousers below the knee to bandage his wound.

"We'll speak later, once we're safe," Raffiel said. "Who knows if that creature will return." He stooped beside Prasus. "How deep is the wound?"

"How deep?" His gray eyebrows shot up. "The bloody thing shot straight through me!" He let out a bitter laugh. "I'll live, though. Didn't hit anything important."

Raffiel looked at where blood wept from beneath Prasus' fingers. It was the outermost part of his left thigh, and Raffiel knew it wasn't a killing blow. Prasus' fae healing had already begun to stymy the bleeding.

Raffiel glanced back at Oliver's body. Even if he was fae, he wouldn't have been able to survive that wound.

"Don't waste your sorrow on him. He summoned those soldiers," Prasus said, seeming to guess Raffiel's line of thought. "He deserved that end."

"Aye," Lysi said. "His life was forfeit the minute he chose to throw that beacon into the sky."

Raffiel shook his head, bile rising in his throat. How much had Oliver been controlled by that witch in his mind? Was he seeing the world through the same haze? It was a terrible feeling, trying to claw back into himself, and he'd wished he'd known sooner, wished he could've been able to save the brown witch.

The sound of drumming horse hooves filled the air once more and they froze.

"What now?" Lysi snarled, searching in the direction of the

horse. Her pointed ears twitched as she listened. "A rider on the main trail, heading southward."

"Wait here," Raffiel said to Prasus.

The elder fae shoved up to a stand with a groan. "I can walk."

Raffiel frowned at him. "Fine, but hang back," he ordered. "Let Lysi and I handle this."

Lysi reached back into her pack and pulled out a length of rope. She looked at Raffiel with a smirk. "I think it's time to hang a washing line."

CHAPTER FIVE

Raffiel and Lysi darted down the narrow trail, unspooling the length of rope between them as they ran. The sound of galloping horse hooves echoed up the ravine. If they hurried, they'd catch the rider at the tight turn and they wouldn't have time to duck the rope.

Raffiel dashed across the path and into the underbrush. He wrapped his end of the rope three times around the tree trunk and then threw the loose end to Lysi. She had to scale the tree to tie the other end high enough. It had to be perfect—too low and the horse would spot it, too high and it would go right over the rider's head.

The beating hooves neared as Lysi dropped from the tree and into the underbrush. They waited, stooped in tense silence as the rider turned the bend—a knight.

A loud crack sounded and the horse whinnied, bolting forward as her rider fell to the ground with a clanging thud. The knight's shout died on his lips as the air knocked out of his lungs.

Raffiel unsheathed his sword, prowling toward the knight. His heart still thundered from the attack, his muscles still coiled in preparation for a sudden assault, and the taste of the heady smoke still clung to the back of his throat. His eyebrows shot up as he surveyed the knight. The soldier wore no insignia, the shining metal of his armor not displaying a single crest or symbol of his patron court.

"Who are you?" Raffiel growled, pointing his sword at the knight.

The flap of the soldier's helmet clinked as he looked at Lysi. Scrambling to his feet, his head twisted toward Raffiel and he froze.

"Does he not speak?" Lysi snarled, advancing a step.

The knight remained frozen for a beat, the eye slits of his helmet staring directly into Raffiel, before he slowly lifted his hand and removed his helmet.

What Raffiel saw made his chest seize—the silver hair, the icy blue eyes, the permanently mischievous smirk. There, standing in the middle of the forest, was Bern Hemarr.

Time seemed to warp as his chest rose and fell, disbelief knitting his eyebrows together.

"Bern?" he whispered, the words barely escaping his lips as warring emotions stung his eyes.

Bern clenched his jaw, his throat bobbing as his eyes welled. He dropped his helmet and in two strides pulled Raffiel into a crushing embrace. Raffiel's shoulder cracked into Bern's armor, but he didn't care, not as he threw his arms around his friend.

"You're alive." Bern's voice was thick as he spoke into the crook of Raffiel's neck. "I found you."

Shock hollowed his voice as he held him, dropping his forehead into Raffiel's shoulder.

Lysi cleared her throat, and the two of them pulled apart. Raffiel wiped under his eyes with his thumb, blinking back the welling tide.

"Lysi, this is my best friend, Bern." Raffiel tried to hide the wobble in his voice and cleared his throat again. He was alive. Bern was alive. Raffiel turned his shocked gaze back to the striking silver-haired fae. "You might be the last of my friends alive."

"Hey," Lysi grumbled.

"Of my old friends," Raffiel snickered. "You're my new friend. Bern, this is Lysi, Prasus' daughter."

"Is Prasus is still alive? That old—" Prasus emerged from the tree line, abruptly cutting off Bern's train of thought. "Oh, he's here." Bern grinned ruefully. "Wonderful."

"Yeah, yeah," Prasus said, pulling Bern into a swift hug. He patted his shoulder, the sound rattling Bern's armor. "I'm glad to see you survived too."

"Where have you been?" Bern looked between the three of them. "All these many years, you've been *alive* and no one found you?"

"We've remained cut off from the outside world," Raffiel said. "Keeping the survivors safe at—"

"Careful," Lysi warned.

Raffiel frowned at her. "We can trust Bern."

"He was a childhood friend, you said." She looked Bern up and down. "How long has it been—six, seven, however many years—since last you saw him? Who knows whose side he's on now?"

"I'm on your side," Bern said, his pale-blue eyes tugging on Raffiel's attention. "Always."

Hairs raised across Raffiel's arm at the sincerity in Bern's voice. He was on Bern's side always too. They had countless misadventures as children. Whenever the high-born fae gathered for weddings and celebrations, Bern's family was invited to attend too. It was one of the many benefits of owning the largest gold mine in Okrith—everyone wanted the Hemarrs to attend their soirees and bring their golden gifts.

Bern still smelled like briny ocean air mixed with lemons and fresh-picked basil—the scent that clung to Silver Sands harbor and which he carried with him wherever he went. The scent tugged on Raffiel's memory with flashes of laughter in the pouring rain, games of knights and bandits, whispered secrets under sheets long after they were meant to be asleep. So young. Still so alive.

Another vivid memory flashed into his mind: the Summer Solstice festival in the Southern Court. He must've been eight at the time. He and Bern had snuck off during the ceremony to go rock pooling on the shoreline. Bern's mother had been furious when she found their salty, wet trousers and tunics caked in sand. Bern had showed him the little Southern snails that clung to the tide pools, how they'd emerge from their shells if you hummed to them. Raffiel had wanted to take a pocketful of them home with him, but Bern had made him toss them back.

"We can trust Bern," Raffiel said with a definitive dip of his chin, wishing he could spend more time in the warm sunlight of that memory. He knew it was true with a surprising certainty. His life was filled with hedged decisions, questioning every choice and outcome, but he was confident from the very depths of his soul—Bern could be trusted.

"You have a camp?" Bern prompted, slinging his arm over Raffiel's shoulder just as he had when they were young. "How many survived the Siege of Yexshire?"

"The campsite is just beyond the High Mountain border to the south," Raffiel continued, ignoring Lysi's huff of bitterness. "There's several hundred, though the numbers are always changing as we find more survivors or High Mountain refugees."

Bern quirked an eyebrow. "That's close to Silver Sands."

"It's a day's walk southward," he replied.

"How have I never heard of this place?"

"We keep to ourselves," Raffiel said. "Only those from the High Mountains."

"And occasionally a stray Western witch," Lysi added with a scowl.

Prasus shifted his weight, grimacing whenever he put pressure on his injured thigh.

"We're heading back to the camp now," Raffiel said, eyeing the injured guard. He turned his hopeful gaze toward Bern. "Join us?"

"Of course." Bern's eyes crinkled at the corners. "I just found you. You think I'm going to just pass on through? No." He clapped Raffiel on the shoulder. "You're stuck with me for a while."

CHAPTER SIX

Once they caught Bern's horse, they cajoled Prasus into riding atop the mare as the descent became steeper. The dappled gray horse was spooked, her ears turning wildly, displeasured snorts coming from her every few minutes. Bern brushed a soothing hand down her side.

"I don't blame her," Lysi muttered. "She probably can sense whatever that witching smoke was back there."

The forest opened to their right, a steep drop to the ravine below. The path cut downward, the trail narrowing, but Bern kept walking beside his horse, whispering calming words to her.

"Bern," Raffiel warned, staring at the edge of Bern's outer boot that hung over the lip of the trail. "Go in front."

"There's space," he insisted.

"Are we going to talk about what just happened?" Lysi scowled. "Or why those soldiers were summoned by that purple smoke?"

Bern leaned past the horse's neck to stare at Lysi. "What?"

"We'll discuss it at the camp," Raffiel said tightly.

He still hadn't decided how much he wanted to tell the others back at their base camp. If he asked Lysi and Prasus to keep it quiet, he knew they would. His people had encountered enough horrors. They didn't need to worry about magic smoke that summoned Northern soldiers too. And then there was the matter of Oliver and his claims. He'd been bewitched by something. Magic? Poison? Both? Whoever that voice was in Raffiel's head was dangerous, and he needed to get to the bottom of who she was. He still felt her clawing at his mind even hours later.

Prasus let out a cough, and the horse whinnied. She bucked, tossing her head to the side and banging into Bern. Bern's arms flailed, circling as Raffiel darted forward to grab his arm. Their wrists locked, but Bern's momentum was too far over the side and, with a yank, they both tumbled over the edge.

Raffiel scrambled against the scrub brush and falling debris, trying to get purchase, but the terrain was too steep. They tumbled head over heels down into the ravine, crashing into the dry river bed at the bottom. He lay on the sun-baked stones, chest heaving, as he looked back up to the top of the ravine. Panic coursed through him numbed his body. It took a few panting breaths before he realized he was uninjured. If the ravine had been only slightly steeper, it probably would've been a lethal fall.

Soon the valley would be filled with a roaring spring river when the snow atop the mountain melted, but barely a trickle currently snaked beneath the stones this far south.

"You alive?" Lysi's voice echoed down from the hilltop.

Raffiel sat up, dusting himself off and glancing at Bern. His silver-haired friend looked queasy and rattled but alive.

"Yeah," Bern grumbled, pulling a twig out of his hair.

Raffiel stumbled to his feet, instantly tripping over again as the world spun.

"Don't bother. You're already in the lowland," Lysi said with a chuckle. "As much as I'd love to see you fall ass over tits again climbing back up here, probably not for the best. We'll meet you at the tree."

Raffiel wiped the back of his hand across his sand-stained brow. "See you there," Raffiel called with a tired wave, watching as they disappeared over the ridge.

"What's the tree?" Bern muttered to Raffiel, dusting away the golden grass clinging to his dented armor.

"It's the encampment just beyond the southern border," Raffiel said with a half-grin. "This fall cut a few hours off our trek today."

"Lucky us." Bern guffawed. "I think I'd prefer the slower descent."

"You should take that armor off." Raffiel eyed where Bern's dented silver armor pressed into his side. "We can bring some people back to retrieve it later. You can't walk with it bent on like that."

"Agreed." Bern sighed as he slowly removed the thin sheets of metal that wrapped around his body. "I'm glad for it, though." He huffed, wiping his hair off his forehead. "I managed to hit every single rock on the way down, which you seemed to avoid."

"I'm very graceful." Raffiel waggled his eyebrows, winning an easy smile from Bern. Raffiel's playful side seemed to be immediately revived with the silver-haired warrior around. When was the last time he had felt like this? And yet, it came so easily with Bern next to him.

Bern's armor clanged unceremoniously to the ground. Raffiel could make out the outline of his muscled body now. The years had made him stronger, broader, having finally grown into his height. Sweat clung to the neckline of Bern's tunic, a peek of muscled shoulder rising from either side of his neck. The sun-kissed hue of his skin was the same shade it had been during all those summertimes they'd spent together, the shade always striking against his pale eyes and hair. No one looked like Bern. Even as a child, Raffiel had thought he must be part God, but now . . . every part of him seemed kissed by the Goddess of Beauty herself.

Bern's lips twisted into a smirk, and Raffiel realized he was staring. He cleared his throat and stooped to grab the chest plate by his feet.

"We can hide it in the scrub brush so no thieves take it," he said.

Bern's hand landed on his arm, halting him. "I can afford new armor."

Raffiel gaped at him. "But this is fine steel."

"My family has more riches than Kings." Bern's eyes softened as if he realized what he was saying. He was certainly richer than the High Mountain King, his body probably still buried beneath the rubble of the Palace of Yexshire.

Raffiel's cheeks burned. He'd spent so many years barely scraping by. He'd forgotten what it felt like to not care whether his boots got holes in them or his weapons rusted, a time when he knew there would always be more. Gods, he'd had no idea what life was really like back then. He'd just want something and there it would be. He promised himself if he ever became King, he wouldn't forget that feeling. His kingdom wouldn't be finished healing until everyone had that certainty—no person would have to fear that if their clothes tore beyond mending, they'd never be able to afford more.

"Why were you riding in full armor anyway?" Raffiel asked, steering the conversation with ease. "The Northern scouts are few and far between these days. It seems hot and uncomfortable to ride with armor, let alone a helmet . . ."

"I didn't want them to see my face," Bern said, kicking aside his greaves with his boot. "It's why I bear no insignia. Traveling through the High Mountains, I want to be a nameless courtier, gallivanting into the woods in his expensive armor just because he can. No one questions a rich fool."

Raffiel snorted. "Very true."

It was the sort of thing he knew courtiers to do—hunting expeditions, quests, travels of self-proclaimed importance, finding ridiculous ways to spend their family's money—it was the sort of thing he'd probably be getting up to now if life had been different.

"Where were you heading that you didn't want people to question?"

"To the red witch camps," Bern said.

Raffiel sucked in a breath through his teeth, the words dousing him in ice. "What?"

"The witch camps," Bern said quizzically. "I heard they were in the northeast. I wanted to see if I could ferry any Southern goods to them. You didn't know?" Raffiel shook his head, his heart thundering. "Raf . . ." Bern's eyes softened. "I think that Rua's with them."

His heart halted, the disbelief stabbing into him so sharply he had to screw his eyes shut. His voice came out as barely a whisper. "She's alive?"

Bern bobbed his head as tears sprung to Raffiel's eyes.

His littlest sister. Images of her tiny freckled face flashed in his mind, the sound of her easy laughter. She was the happiest child, a lively shining spirit.

His breath caught in his throat. "She's alive."

Bern took a step forward, pulling Raffiel into a tight hug. His arms instinctively wrapped around him, relishing the feeling of Bern's warm chest pressed against his own, so much better than holding him with armor on. He folded into Bern, letting his friend hold him as tears of relief trailed down his cheeks. He wasn't the only one still alive. Rua had survived.

"How did you know of the camp?" Raffiel's voice muffled into Bern's tunic.

Bern chuckled. "You're going to think I'm crazy." Raffiel pulled away, a question on his face. "Baba Morganna spoke to me in a dream."

"What?" Raffiel searched Bern's eyes. "Baba is alive as well? How many survived?"

"Dozens, maybe more. She showed me images of the camp," Bern said. "I think she has the blue witches' gift of Sight now, along with her red witch magic . . . but I've never seen a witch project into dreams before."

"Are you certain this wasn't just a normal dream?" Raffiel shifted nervously, thinking of the scratchy voice that had whispered into his own mind that day.

"It wasn't." Bern gave a confident nod. "It was real. I'm going to find them."

"Then I'm coming too," Raffiel said, turning and heading uphill.

"Raf," Bern called after him with a laugh. "Wait, we need to get back to your camp first."

"If Rua's alive, I need to find her. Now."

"You're not thinking sensibly," Bern grumbled, chasing after him as he broke into a jog.

Bern cut in front of Raffiel, halting his hillside ascent. His pale blue eyes stared daggers into him, and the weight of those eyes made him rock back on his heels.

"I need to see her," Raffiel whispered, emotions constricting his throat.

"I know." Bern's voice was a steady, deep rumble. "I will lead you to her, but first, we need provisions. We're less than a day from your camp. We need horses." He looked over Raffiel's shoulder toward his discarded armor. "And better disguises."

"We don't—"

"We do," Bern cut him off, seeming to already know what he was going to say. "Do you want to lead the North straight into their camp? Are you willing to reveal their hiding place?" Bern took a step closer, his chest brushing against Raffiel's as his warm breath brushed his cheek. "Don't ask me to risk them catching you, not when I've only just learned that you're alive."

"Fine," Raffiel gritted out as he dropped Bern's heated gaze. "That was a manipulative thing to say."

Bern grinned. "I don't care as long as it worked."

"We return to camp for provisions and then you take me to the witches, agreed?" Raffiel narrowed his eyes at Bern until the courtier nodded. "Good."

"There's that princely tone I know and love," Bern taunted, elbowing Raffiel as he trudged back downhill.

The words flickered like an ember in his chest. "I was arrogant and selfish back then."

"No, you weren't," Bern snickered, following a pace behind, hopping from stone to stone down the vigorless river bed. "I think you have a skewed memory of yourself."

"I don't think a princely tone suits me anymore," Raffiel muttered.

"I agree," Bern said. "You're better suited to a kingly tone now." Raffiel gave him a look over his shoulder before carrying on. "What?" Bern laughed, a deep, hearty sound that made Raffiel's stomach flip. "I'm right. You can be a humble ruler and a confident one. Your people need your assurance, your leadership, as much as they need your kindness. It is brave to lead the people who have followed you, whether you wanted them to or not."

"Always with the wise words, Bern." Raffiel chuckled.

"It's gotten worse with age."

Raffiel smiled. He didn't realize how much he missed this until he had it again. Everyone around him held him at arm's length. He was their future King; they listened to him, even revered him, but there was no taunting, no lighthearted jabs or pushing. Only Prasus and Lysi dared speak to him like a friend. But now his oldest friend was alive, and his sister too . . .

The tightness in his chest eased, replaced by an airy lightness that terrified him. It felt like free-falling, his stomach lifting into his throat, weightless. For the first time in a long time, he felt it—hope.

CHAPTER SEVEN

As they walked southward, the strange magic of the Southern Court pulled on them as the temperatures started to rise. The frigid, snow-capped landscapes of the High Mountains morphed into teeming, humid jungles in only the span of an hour. The air was so thick, it was hard to breathe.

"Gods," Raffiel cursed, wiping his tunic sleeve across his sweaty forehead.

"You High Mountain fae can't handle the Southern heat," Bern teased.

"It never gets easier." Raffiel scowled at Bern's rosy cheeks, only the thinnest sheen of sweat on his brow. "It's not even summer in the South yet."

"Let's break." Bern nodded toward the rocks on the banks of the dry riverbed. "I'm thirsty."

"You're saying that just for my benefit." Raffiel huffed, fanning himself.

"Maybe."

They stooped on two smooth rocks, worn from the roaring rivers that would sweep downhill come summer. Raffiel took a long swig of his water skin and passed it to Bern.

"How much farther?" Bern asked.

"Two hours, maybe less," Raffiel said, mopping his sweaty

face again. He grumbled at his sweat-stained tunic and whipped it over his head.

"Curse the moon." Bern gaped at Raffiel's muscled bare chest. "What are they feeding you at this camp?"

Raffiel chuckled. "Training. Time."

Bern's gaze dropped down to the rusted sword on Raffiel's hip. "We need to get you a proper weapon. That is no sword to be leading armies with."

The word *we* stuck in Raffiel's mind. He paused, the warmth of his smile not meeting his eyes. "After we find Rua, you need to head back to Silver Sands."

Bern's brow dropped heavy over his icy blue eyes. "No."

"You are a high-born fae of noble standing," Raffiel insisted. "You still have a place in the world."

"I only just found you."

"You put yourself in unnecessary danger by being near me."

Bern's face darkened, his gaze hard. "Unnecessary?"

"I just mean—"

"No," Bern cut him off. "Whatever you're trying to say, just stop. I'm not saying goodbye to you again." Panic gripped his voice, his thoughts streaming out of his mouth, one sentence faster than the next. "You *need* someone like me, someone well-connected, someone still a part of the world. I can help you and your people. You've been cut off from the world for too long. I can be the perfect spy. They think I only care about gold mines and wine."

"Easy," Raffiel said as if calming a skittish horse. "I just . . . I don't want you to have to sacrifice like I have."

"Do you think I couldn't live without the parties and the wine?" Bern laughed bitterly. "Do you think my family would even miss me? There's only one person who's ever felt like family to me . . ."

Raffiel's heart thundered in his chest and he knew he couldn't blame it on the hiking. His burning cheeks were not from the Southern heat. It was true: of all the people in his life, of all the ones who loved him, there was only one that he felt tied to more than any other, as if half of his soul existed in someone else. The same thoughts, the same jokes, someone who knew when he was angry or sad before he even knew it himself.

Raffiel reached out and lifted Bern's chin until those ice blue eyes met his own. "I missed you," he whispered.

Bern's throat bobbed, his lips parting as his eyes roved Raffiel's face. "I missed you too."

Raffiel sucked in a sharp breath, the pain of having mourned the fae in front of him now panging through him anew. He didn't want to lose him again. Couldn't.

Bern shot his hand out, cupping Raffiel around the back of his neck, pulling Raffiel's mouth to his waiting lips. Raffiel snaked his arms around Bern's back, pulling him closer until his bare chest fused with the fabric of Bern's tunic. Lightning shot through his limbs. The feeling of those lips was the most potent sort of magic. It buzzed through him, his heart leaping at the soft groans and the fingertips pressing into his flesh.

How many years had he wanted to do this? How long had his every secret moment of desire been perfectly honed to the fae who was kissing him now?

His hands fisted into Bern's tunic, desperate to be closer. He sucked on Bern's bottom lip, licking his tongue into his mouth and tasting him. Perfect. The strong taste of Silver Sands, the sea-salt air and zest of lemons. Raffiel's tongue worked across Bern's, a deep moan pulling from his lungs.

A loud whinny yanked them apart. Bern's hand shot to the hilt of his sword as he scanned the gorge. Raffiel's chest heaved, sucking humid air through his panting lips.

"Scouts?" he whispered, straining his ears for the sound of horse hooves.

"They're riding up the far bank," Bern whispered back. "Go hide in the bushes."

"What?"

"Go hide." He shoved Raffiel's shoulder, nodding toward the waxy-leafed bushes beyond the river bank. "They won't bother me. Go."

Raffiel gave him a warning look, knowing Bern would understand what it meant: don't do something foolish. Bern gave him a cavalier wink, and Raffiel darted off into the bushes. He stooped behind the thick branches, peeking out through a gap in the foliage.

Three rider-mounted horses wandered the soft earth beyond the rocky river banks. They had scraggily beards, threadbare clothes, and the hollow eyes of those who smoked too much of the Southern witching brew. The empty, blood-stained sacks tied to their saddle bags told Raffiel enough. They were witch hunters.

"Greetings." Bern bowed to them as if he were welcoming royalty to a ball.

"Who are you?" The tallest one cocked his head at Bern, roving from his expensive leather boots to his pointed fae ears. "And what are you doing out here?"

"I'm Bern Hemarr," he said with the grin that always made Raffiel's gut clench.

The witch hunter scratched at his copper-red beard. "The heir to the gold mines in Silver Sands?"

Bern puffed his chest up. "One in the same."

The witch hunter considered Bern for a moment, his eyes wandering past him and into the forest. Raffiel grimaced when the witch hunter's eyes landed directly on him.

"Got a maiden with ya?" he asked, narrowing his eyes at the bush.

Raffiel folded his hands over his chest as if hiding breasts and ducked lower as the three witch hunters chuckled.

"Can you blame me?" Bern laughed along with them.

"A tavern girl?" His eyes turned predatory. "A witch?"

"Unfortunately, not." Bern maintained his easy tone. "She's a fae of some note and, I must say, I would be in terrible trouble with the North if she became the subject of gossip."

The witch hunters' faces turned wary, even their horses taking a step backward as if sensing the threat. No one messed with the Northern fae. Angering Hennen Vostemur was the worst fate a person could bestow on themselves since the Siege of Yexshire. And these witch hunters needed Vostemur's gold.

"Aye, well, we'll leave you to it," the red-bearded one said with a bob of his head. He coaxed his horse onward, the other two witch hunters touching their foreheads in a sign of respect as they rode away.

Raffiel waited, huddled behind the bushes until his fae hearing could no longer detect the clomping hooves.

"You see?" Bern swiveled around and grinned at Raffiel as he emerged from the forest. "I'm a useful person to keep around."

Raffiel huffed, grabbing his tunic from the rock and carrying on down the path. "You most certainly are."

He wanted to stop, wanted to kiss Bern again and see where that kiss led. He touched his swollen lips, listening to Bern whistle as he walked a pace behind him. Raffiel had thought about it so many times in the years since their parting —what would it have been like to kiss that silver-haired boy with the charming smile. He'd thought he'd never get the chance and, even if he did, that Bern wouldn't reciprocate his affections. But now looking back, he should've known. Every look, every hug, every lingering touch, he'd wondered if Bern felt the same . . . now he knew for certain.

CHAPTER EIGHT

Raffiel yanked his tunic back over his head, and Bern's whistling halted.

"Must you?" Bern teased.

Raffiel glanced over his shoulder, a wolflike grin spreading across his face in mirror to Bern's own. He couldn't believe it. After all this time, Bern felt the same way. In some regards, it felt like no time had passed, like they had picked back up mid-conversation after all these many years, but there were cracks in their souls now too. The years hadn't been kind. So many horrors had transpired and so many people had died. The lightness of Bern's presence lifted a weight off Raffiel that he hadn't realized he'd been carrying, only now feeling its sudden absence.

"Not very kingly," Raffiel said, "if I stroll into camp shirtless."

"Oh, I don't know about that." Bern chuckled as Raffiel's feet seemed to stop of their own volition. He stared down the trail. "What's wrong?"

"Nothing."

"What kind of nothing?"

"It gets harder. Every time I return - ..." Raffiel swallowed. "Every time I see the camp and all those people who look to me like I will make everything better, as if I have the answers to their salvation."

Bern wandered closer. "That is a lot to carry."

"I've always felt one step from breaking apart." Raffiel let out a shuddering breath. He hadn't spoken of this to anyone, not even Prasus, though he suspected the soldier could see it in his eyes. But with Bern, with that ease his old friend brought him, he finally said it aloud. "I don't know if I can do this."

In two steps, Bern was there. "You *can* do this." Bern put his arm around his shoulder as Raffiel swallowed back the tears and whispered, "Maybe the Gods knew our paths needed to cross again. Maybe they watched us as children and knew there's nothing we couldn't carry between the two of us."

Raffiel looked into those pale blue eyes and already the words were on the tip of his tongue: he loved him. He'd always loved him. He knew it with more certainty than he knew his own name. But knowing something and speaking it were two very different things. That day would come for them, hopefully, maybe, if the Gods were kind. Raffiel turned his head into Bern's shoulder and let Bern stroke a soothing hand down his back.

"Come on," Bern murmured. "Introduce me to your people."

It took more strength than he'd care to admit to release Bern and keep walking. Each of Bern's footsteps sounding down the path behind Raffiel steadied him. He rolled his shoulders back and lifted his chin, preparing to face his people once more.

They were so close to the camp that Raffiel smelled the cooking wafting on the humid air. He wondered if Prasus and Lysi were already there and if the rest of the camp had been well. How was the elderly blue witch and her bad knee? How would she fare with the monsoons finally ebbing to the hot spring days? He knew each of their names, and each of their stories, his future intertwined with their own. Raffiel had always thought Kings led through strength and pride, but it was that quiet concern, that humbling reflection, that he knew his people truly needed.

Lost in his thoughts, it wasn't until Bern unsheathed his sword that he heard it—thundering horse hooves.

Raffiel frantically searched the forest. What were riders doing in this part of the jungle? It was too thick, the paths too narrow, most riders were deterred from heading in this direction.

"Run into the forest," Bern gritted out, shoving Raffiel, but it was too late.

It happened so fast. Shouting rang out as he grabbed his rusty sword. Two Northern soldiers, resplendent in shining silver armor came barreling down the trail, two more behind them. They rode giant black horses with braided manes and massive shaggy hooves. The front soldier was swinging at Bern before he even got a good look at him.

Bern's sword clanged against the rider's. The soldier's sword slid up Bern's blocked arm, slicing him up the side of his neck to his jaw.

Raffiel bellowed out a panicked yell, blocking another strike as Bern dropped to his knees.

"Halt!" a cold voice snapped from the farthest horse.

Raffiel's stomach turned to acid as he caught a flash of that ash-blond hair, the perfectly starched white tunic, and shined riding boots. He lifted his gaze and locked eyes with none other than Renwick Vostemur, The Witchslayer.

Time seemed to freeze as those emerald green eyes pierced into him. That moment in the inferno, the split second in the castle in Yexshire—Raffiel knew Renwick was thinking of the same.

The Northern Crown Prince had turned on his own guards in the melee, feigning confusion, while Raffiel escaped out a window. As the years passed and he earned his new moniker, The Witchslayer, Raffiel had wondered if it was a false memory. But now, staring into those wary emerald eyes, he knew it was true. The Witchslayer had saved him that night.

Bern's groan pulled him from the memory and he whirled, stooping to see the bloodied hand Bern held to his neck.

"It's not deep," he rasped, blood trickling from his fingers.

"Liar," Raffiel hissed. "We need to get to the healers."

The camp was just through the forest.

"I'm okay," Bern said with a soft smirk. "Really. I think I'll look good with a scar."

Raffiel narrowed his eyes at him. "Only you would say that after you almost had your throat slit."

"You're . . . You're the Dammacus Prince!" the front guard said, mouth agape. "Your Highness," he called to Renwick. "We've found him at last!"

"Thador," Renwick muttered to the giant fae warrior beside him. It was all he needed to say, and the massive guard dismounted and called for the other two soldiers to do the same.

"Raf, run!" Bern shouted, leaping to his feet and holding out his sword even as he kept his other clamped to his neck.

Thador advanced, yanking his dagger from the belt on his thigh. In one swift movement, he raised his dagger . . . and plunged it into his own guard's throat.

"Wh-what are you—" The second soldier's voice morphed into wet gurgles as Thador turned his blade on him.

The two Northern soldiers collapsed, blood pouring from their necks, their armor rattling as they slammed into the soil.

Raffiel stared at Thador and then to Renwick. The Northern Prince's eyes held no emotion, sharp and assessing as he looked at the bodies of his own guards.

"They disappeared into the Southern jungles on our way west." Renwick's voice was cold but steady. "They never returned." Thador nodded, wiping his blade on his trouser leg before sheathing it again.

Renwick turned his emerald eyes on them, so young and so hollow, the same haunted look as Oliver, and Raffiel wondered if he'd been hearing whisperings too.

"We're off to Silver Sands . . ." Renwick scanned Bern from head to toe. "You were there the whole time. Thank you for your hospitality, Bern."

Bern's shoulders slumped in relief. "It was a lovely visit, Your Highness."

Renwick's gaze flicked to Raffiel. "There's no one in the eastern mountains . . . we've searched thoroughly." He said the words slowly, carefully. "So there will be no Northern soldiers on the eastern trails, should you wish to go see its emptiness for yourself."

Raffiel's eyes flared. Did he know about the witch camp in the eastern mountains? Did he know Rua was there?

Raffiel swallowed. "Thank you."

"Don't thank me," Renwick gritted out, the muscle in his jaw flickering. His eyes dropped to the bodies on the ground. "I have earned the title of Witchslayer a hundred times over. Do not *thank* me."

Raffiel saw it all in him now—how much Renwick hated himself. He'd been quiet and standoffish, even when they were children, but he wore his loathing like armor now. He had dark circles under his eyes, a vacant, angry expression. There had been a time when they were young—Raffiel, Hale, Renwick, Bern—when they had all been friends. They'd spar with wooden swords at Solstice ceremonies and sneak sips of witches' wine from moon altars. They'd planned to marry their children to each other's, start new royal families, make new sweeping changes for the betterment of their kingdoms—lofty ideals that would never come to pass. It hurt more than he'd care to admit, releasing that hope.

"Keep the horses," Renwick said, his only farewell, and he and Thador turned and rode off in the direction from which they came.

Raffiel watched with sad eyes as that ash-blond hair disappeared through the forest, and he wondered if he'd ever seen his former friend again.

"That was . . ." Bern stared down at the bodies and then over at the horses grazing the dense foliage.

Raffiel's eyes drifted out of focus, his gaze hooked on the forest trail. It wasn't until his eyes were burning that he blinked. "That was the second time the Witchslayer saved my life."

CHAPTER NINE

The first person to spot them was a little boy at the edge of camp. His eyes widened as large as saucers when he spotted Raffiel, and, rather than greeting the Prince, he dashed back through the jungle shouting the news.

Bern chuckled. "Whether it's on gilded carriages or trudging through the jungle, a royal reception is always the same." He clapped Raffiel on the back, his fingers lingering on the mound of his shoulder muscle and squeezing.

Raffiel knew what it meant: I'm here. It'll be okay.

He took a steeling breath, cutting through the new overgrown weeds and pulling back carefully placed branches to hide their trail. The dense jungle easily obscured the camp. They ducked under the vines and stumbled through the leaves until the forest opened up to a large clearing. Canvas huts circled a fire pit ringed in log benches. Clothes hung on washing lines strung between the dwellings, and repurposed wood scraps lined overflowing garden beds beneath. People hustled about carrying baskets of foraged tropical fruits and bundles of firewood.

The bustle of midday halted when they spotted Raffiel. Broad smiles and warm relief greeted him as he returned. The crowd converged, bowing and hugging him as he passed through the tightening throng and toward a person waiting on the other side of the clearing.

Prasus sat propped against the lean trunk of a broad-leafed tree. Bern's horse grazed the edge of the forest beside him.

"You made it back in one piece, I see," Prasus said with an approving nod. He glanced at the wound down Bern's neck. "You, not so much."

"Shouldn't I be saying that to you?" Raffiel eyed Prasus' bandaged leg. "How bad is it?"

"He'll be fine in a week or two," Lysi said from behind them. She carried two leaves mounded with wild rice and stir-fried vegetables. She passed one to her father and crouched beside him, picking at the lunch with her fingers. She hummed as she licked her fingertips. "May all the Gods bless the green witches."

Bern whirled around to stare at the witches standing over the fire pit in the center of the clearing. "You have green witches here?"

"They were residing in Yexshire when the attack happened," Lysi said with a shrug. "They fled here with us."

"But surely they could return to the green witch coven here in the South?" Bern cocked his head.

"They're High Mountain people," Raffiel insisted. "Regardless of what color their magic is, Yexshire is as much their homeland as it is mine. They wanted to stay."

Bern considered the witch stirring the blackened pot hanging above the flames. Another beside her passed out food as children carried more leaves over.

The High Mountain Court had always been a place where humans, fae, and witches from all over Okrith gathered. It was one of the many things about their court that Hennen Vostemur didn't like. He feared a world where witches weren't tied to royal fae, where they could move and intermingle as they saw fit. It made it much harder to hate someone when you couldn't define what they were.

"How is the camp?" Raffiel turned back to Prasus and Lysi. "How is everyone faring?"

"No casualties," Prasus said through a mouthful of food.

"Sabine had her baby," Lysi said with a soft smile. "They're both doing well."

Raffiel grinned. "I'm glad. We should go congratulate her."

"How many have you lost?" Bern asked.

They all looked at him, their faces growing vacant as they considered how many people they tried to rescue that didn't make it to this place. How many times had Raffiel promised an oasis away from witch hunters and Northern soldiers and not been able to lead them to it? Those early years, the mountains were rife with them. Each of their excursions to find survivors had been treacherous, the earth stained red with blood. Too many lives were lost.

"You should take him to the tree," Lysi said quietly, not meeting Raffiel's eyes.

"The tree?" Bern asked.

Raffiel looked at his feet and said, "Come on."

They stumbled farther through the forest, Bern silent at Raffiel's back. He seemed to understand that they were entering a hallowed space. When the forest cleared, he felt Bern's gasp like an arrow to the back. That sound would live within him forever.

The sight never became easier to take in.

Raffiel stared at the ancient, gnarled tree, its branches laden with crimson red ribbons. They waved softly in the wind as if ghostly hands lifted them. A shallow numbness spread through him as he stepped forward.

"What is this place?" Bern's voice was barely a whisper.

"A prayer tree," Raffiel murmured back. "One lone red ribbon hung on the tree when we discovered it."

He remembered that jarring sight: the red fabric had looked ripped from a cloak, the long strip tied on the lowest knobby branch. Now, the branches could barely be seen through the thick waves of red.

Bern stumbled forward. "How many have you hung up?"

"Too many," Raffiel said, stooping to a bundle of ribbon loosely wound together. He pulled the knife from his belt and cut a length of ribbon. Bern looked at him, a question on his face. "For Oliver."

Bern nodded and watched as Raffiel stepped up to the tree and whispered his soft fae prayers. Bern walked around the tree, his fingers trailing the streams of red as Raffiel prayed. When the prayer was finished, Raffiel hung the ribbon and walked around to Bern.

Tears welled in Bern's eyes as he took in the sight. "I know for certain now I was meant to find you." He turned toward Raffiel and put his hand to the center of Raffiel's chest. "Can you feel it?"

Raffiel clenched his jaw, covering Bern's hand with his own, too overcome with emotions to speak as he nodded.

"Do you know what it means?" Bern's eyes searched his own, the word whispering into Raffiel's mind as if Bern spoke it himself.

A tear slid down his cheek. "Yes."

At the sight of that tear, Bern pulled him into a searing kiss. His mouth fused with Bern's, breathing in his essence as that kiss tingled across his skin.

It was real. He was real. His Fated.

Raffiel pulled back, resting his forehead against Bern's. He panted, their breaths intermingling and that sweet, salt-air taste still on his tongue. Raffiel brushed one more soft kiss on Bern's full lips and pulled away, turning toward the tree. He found a short length of ribbon, its edges frayed, the sun bleaching it of color. He reached up and untied it.

Clenching it in his fist, he turned to Bern and said, "Let's go find Rua."

Thank you for reading Raffiel's story! ℔

you enjoyed The Witching Trail, please consider leaving a review, sharing on social media, or telling a friend! -A.K. xx

you enjoyed The Witching Trail, please consider leaving a review, sharing on social media, or telling a friend! -A.K. xx

THE SERPENT AND THE OASIS

Through the mountains high and low,
A red witch wandered, lost and alone,
Until a serpent she did spy,
Crimson and sleek, it caught her eye.

"Follow me," it hissed and went,
The frightened witch did relent,
Over Mount Seripedes they did go,
Through hail and wind and freezing snow.

But the snake was true to its word,
And led the witch to safety, undeterred,
To a land of fruit trees and golden sunshine
And a breeze filled with scents so divine

So heed this tale, for goodness sake,
When lost, follow the crimson snake,
And you too may find your way,
To see the dawn of a brand new day.

PATREON

Join A. K. Mulford's Patreon to receive ARCs, book mail, access to the Mountaineers discord server, spicy artwork, and brand new novellas!

ACKNOWLEDGMENTS

Thank you to all of my amazing patrons for making this novella possible! I love creating worlds with you!

A very special thank you to my fae and royal fae patrons: Jaime, Linda, Nicole, Leslie, Marissa, Traci, Amy, Ciara, Drea, Hannah, Kelly, Maggie, Mandy, Mariah, Sarah, Shanda, and Virginia. Your support means so much to me! I can't wait to take you on more adventures in Okrith!

Thank you to Sara from Sara Dawn Johnson editing!

Thank you to the amazing Kate for formatting the paperbacks of these novellas and running the A.K. merch shop!

Thank you to Holly Dunn for the design for the Map of Okrith and thank you to MiblArt for the cover design.

ABOUT THE AUTHOR

A.K. Mulford is a bestselling fantasy author and former wildlife biologist who swapped rehabilitating monkeys for writing novels.

She/they are inspired to create diverse stories that transport readers to new realms, making them fall in love with fantasy for the first time, or, all over again.

She now lives in Australia with her husband and two young human primates, creating lovable fantasy characters and making ridiculous Tiktok videos.

www.akmulford.com

ALSO BY AK MULFORD

The Okrith Novellas

The Witch of Crimson Arrows

The Witch Apothecary

The Witchslayer

The Witching Trail

The Witch's Goodbye

The Five Crowns Of Okrith Series

The High Mountain Court

The Witches' Blade

The Rogue Crown

The Evergreen Heir

The Amethyst Kingdom

The Golden Court Series

A River of Golden Bones

A Sky of Emerald Stars